# Hodder Toddler

## This book belongs to:

....................................................

*In memory of my mother*
*Katherine Y.K. Su, with love*

LITTLE SUNBEAM

by Lucy Su

British Library Cataloguing in Publication Data

A catalogue record of this book is available from the British Library.

ISBN 0 340 79535 2 (PB)

Copyright © Lucy Su 2001

The right of Lucy Su to be identified as the author and illustrator

of this Work has been asserted by her in accordance with

the Copyright, Designs and Patents Act 1988.

First edition published 2001

10 9 8 7 6 5 4 3

Published by Hodder Children's Books

a division of Hodder Headline Limited

338 Euston Road London NW1 3BH

Printed in Hong Kong

# Little Sunbeam

## Lucy Su

Hodder
Children's
Books

A division of Hodder Headline Limited

It was a warm summer's evening.
A sunbeam floated into Baby's bedroom
while the baby played outside.

Something caught the sunbeam's eye.
It settled down for a nap.

# Bump!
Baby woke up!
There was something
under the cupboard!

What was it?
Baby couldn't quite reach.

Suddenly it shot
past Baby and hid
behind the curtains.

Slowly Baby pulled them back.
Oh! It was a little sunbeam.

The sun had gone
last night and left
the sunbeam all alone.

But now the sky was getting light. The sun had begun to rise. It was nearly morning.

The sunbeam wanted to go home. Baby looked for something to help.

Now what could
be done with
these?

Push. **Whoops.** No good!

Up

and

down.

But what
was that on
the shelf?

I can get it!

Much better.

The sunbeam
squeezed in.

Home to the sun, little sunbeam!